. . . and so is the *Death Pudding!*

Cue flashing lights and sound FX:
Ba-ba-ba-boom!

Can the world be saved?

Over to the kids at Plumpot Primary . . .

Jeremy Strong once worked in a bakery, putting the jam into three thousand doughnuts every night. Now he puts the jam in stories instead, which he finds much more exciting. At the age of three, he fell out of a first-floor bedroom window and landed on his head. His mother says that this damaged him for the rest of his life and refuses to take any responsibility. He loves writing stories because he says it is 'the only time you alone have complete control and can make anything happen'. His ambition is to make you laugh (or at least snuffle). Jeremy Strong lives near Bath with four cats and a flying cow.

Are you feeling silly enough to read more?

THE HUNDRED-MILE-AN-HOUR DOG
RETURN OF THE HUNDRED-MILE-AN-HOUR DOG
WANTED! THE HUNDRED-MILE-AN-HOUR DOG

MY DAD'S GOT AN ALLIGATOR!
MY GRANNY'S GREAT ESCAPE
MY MUM'S GOING TO EXPLODE!
MY BROTHER'S FAMOUS BOTTOM
MY BROTHER'S FAMOUS BOTTOM GETS PINCHED!

BEWARE! KILLER TOMATOES
CHICKEN SCHOOL
I'M TELLING YOU, THEY'RE ALIENS
KRAZY KOW SAVES THE WORLD – WELL, ALMOST

LAUGH YOUR SOCKS OFF WITH

Jeremy STRONG

Invasion of the Christmas Puddings

Illustrated by

Rowan Clifford

PUFFIN

PUFFIN BOOKS

Published by the Penguin Group
Penguin Books Ltd, 80 Strand, London WC2R 0RL, England
Penguin Group (USA) Inc., 375 Hudson Street, New York, New York 10014, USA
Penguin Group (Canada), 90 Eglinton Avenue East, Suite 700, Toronto, Ontario, Canada M4P 2Y3
(a division of Pearson Penguin Canada Inc.)
Penguin Ireland, 25 St Stephen's Green, Dublin 2, Ireland (a division of Penguin Books Ltd)
Penguin Group (Australia), 250 Camberwell Road, Camberwell, Victoria 3124, Australia
(a division of Pearson Australia Group Pty Ltd)
Penguin Books India Pvt Ltd, 11 Community Centre, Panchsheel Park, New Delhi – 110 017, India
Penguin Group (NZ), 67 Apollo Drive, Rosedale, North Shore 0632, New Zealand
(a division of Pearson New Zealand Ltd)
Penguin Books (South Africa) (Pty) Ltd, 24 Sturdee Avenue, Rosebank, Johannesburg 2196, South Africa

Penguin Books Ltd, Registered Offices: 80 Strand, London WC2R 0RL, England

puffinbooks.com

First published 2007
5

Text copyright © Jeremy Strong, 2007
Illustrations copyright © Rowan Clifford, 2007
All rights reserved

Set in 14/23pt MT Baskerville
Made and printed in England by Clays Ltd, St Ives plc

British Library Cataloguing in Publication Data
A CIP catalogue record for this book is available from the British Library

ISBN: 978-0-141-32320-6

www.greenpenguin.co.uk

Penguin Books is committed to a sustainable future
for our business, our readers and our planet.
The book in your hands is made from paper
certified by the Forest Stewardship Council.

For Gillie, who has longer than average arms and a larger than average heart, with thanks for all the suggestions, the laughter, and the Moments

CONTENTS

ONE:
IN THE
BEGINNING . . .

They gathered at the furthest reaches
of the known universe – millions of
them. What were they? Christmas
puddings. Why were they gathering
there? They were preparing to invade
PLANET EARTH.

*DANGG DUH-DANGG DANGG
– SPLURRPP!!*

But where had they come from? An unknown universe on *The Other Side*. It is true. Beyond our universe is another, and like a mirror it reflects everything we know and see. It is known to scientists as a universe of the fifth dimension.

 Our science expert, Professor Dump-Crumpett, explains:

'Oh, please, this is easy-squeezy. There are many dimensions. Imagine a box. Look at the box. You can already see three dimensions. Firstly there is Width. How wide is the box? Secondly there is Height. How high is the box? The third dimension is Depth. How deep is the box? The fourth dimension is Time. Look at the box. Here it is now, but where was it yesterday? You couldn't see it, because you weren't reading this book. But it was here! The fifth dimension is Reflection, or The Other Side. There is another box, like the first one. But it is not in this book. It is in another book, like this one, but on The Other Side. If we can't see it how do we know it is there? WE DON'T! But we suspect it is, just as you are there when you look in a mirror. We have never seen The Other Side. But it IS there. That's enough for now. Goodbye!'

And so the puddings came through from The Other Side. No, they didn't simply *come* through – they *poured* through in their hundreds of thousands, in their millions.

MILLIONS OF CHRISTMAS PUDDINGS.
And they were made of . . .
STICKY MATTER!
Beyond the reach of our most powerful

telescopes, at the far edge of our universe, the puddings gathered, hovering in dark outer space. But WHO, or WHAT, was behind this deadly invasion? Somewhere a dark shadow shifted among the distant stars. An evil force was slipping into our world, bringing with him a terrifying invasion force of Christmas puddings. And very soon Earth would fall!

DANGG DUH-DANGG DANGG – SPLURRPP!!
(Again.)

ONE AND A HALF: MEANWHILE BACK ON EARTH . . .

Father Christmas was cross. He had just managed to set fire to his slippers. Fortunately Mrs Christmas was nearby and she prevented the slippers from setting the house ablaze by snatching them up with the salad tongs. She plunged the flaming footwear into the sink, where they hissed, spat and sank out of sight.

'What on earth did you think you were doing?' she shouted.

'I was trying to warm them up,' cried Father Christmas with exasperation.

'IN THE TOASTER?!' yelled Mrs Christmas. 'You daft tomato! You can't warm slippers in the toaster!'

'Why not? Daft tomato yourself!' Father

Christmas bellowed back.

'Bread goes in the toaster, not slippers!' cried Mrs Christmas. 'Why put slippers in the toaster?'

'Because my feet are COLD!' roared Father Christmas. 'And I don't like cold slippers. It's like wearing fish on your feet.'

'And how often do you wear fish on your feet?' yelled Mrs Christmas.

'Didn't say I did. Said it was *like* wearing fish on

your feet. It would be like putting your feet inside a large haddock.'

'And why would anyone want to imagine putting their feet inside a haddock, large or small?' Mrs Christmas went on, pulling her husband's slippers from the washing-up bowl and putting them into the bin. 'You crazy cauliflower.'

'I'm imagining it so that I can explain why I don't like cold slippers,' Father Christmas snapped back. 'And you're a brainless banana.'

Mrs Christmas put her enormous hands on her equally enormous hips and glared at her husband. Father Christmas glared back. A moment later the room exploded with laughter. Mrs Christmas collapsed back into a chair, which put considerable strain on its creaking legs, while her husband rocked on his feet. He at last managed to stop laughing long enough to tell his wife that what he wanted for Christmas, more than anything else, was –

'A new pair of slippers!' she spluttered and they

collapsed into hysterics again.

Father Christmas pulled on his boots, still chuckling to himself. He paused for a moment and a frown slowly appeared on his forehead.

'Why is there only one day for Christmas? It's so much work. I've got parcels coming out of my ears. Other people get the whole year to do things. I get one day. And that's a holiday for everyone, except me. It's not fair.'

'There, there, calm down, my big red jellybean. At least you have your lovely new sleigh.'

They gazed out at the fabulously shiny rocket-sleigh. An overnight frosting of snow had given the ship a magical glitter.

Father Christmas slipped a loving arm round his wife's waist – or at least he slipped his arm round as much of it as he could manage, considering her size – and his.

Meanwhile Mrs Christmas carried on knitting the cardigan she was wearing. It had a habit of unravelling at the bottom because she didn't know how to cast off. The consequence was that she spent half her time knitting back what had unravelled. She had to keep a ball of wool and needles with her all the time. Unfortunately she didn't have pockets on her cardigan because she hadn't knitted them yet, and there were no pockets on her skirt, so she stuck the ball of wool on her head and held it in place with the needles.

'It's pretty smart, isn't it?' he murmured happily.

'Yes, my gigantic mince pie. You can leave the reindeer behind this year and they can have a rest.

Shall I give you a hand with loading up?'

'Not if you do what you did last year,' grunted Father Christmas.

'And what was that?' asked Mrs Christmas frostily.

'You didn't tie on the sacks properly. I was halfway across America when I had to take sharp action to avoid a space shuttle and a sack fell off. It crashed to Earth and completely demolished a truck carrying baked beans. You can imagine the mess that made. The worst of it was that I had to come all the way back home to pick up another sack, and it was all your fault.'

'It wasn't. You probably braked too quickly.'

'Braked? Reindeer can't brake, you daft jam pot! The best they can do is slow down.'

'Then you shouldn't have been driving so fast,' sniffed Mrs Christmas.

'But I had the whole world to get round in one day! I can't dawdle. Honestly, sometimes I think your brain has been boiled in a pan for a week.'

'Why do you need to load up now, anyway? It's days before Christmas is upon us.'

Father Christmas groaned. He had explained this three times already. 'I need to test the new sleigh. I want to see how it performs with a full load. If there are any problems I want to know about them now, not on Christmas Day.'

Mrs Christmas nudged him with a fat elbow. 'Go on! You just want to have a whizz round in your new toy. You're a boy racer at heart, that's what you are. I suppose you'll miss lunch too. I'll make you some sandwiches.'

ONE AND THREE-QUARTERS AT MUCH THE SAME TIME, IN BRITAIN . . .

Miss Comet was the youngest, prettiest and nicest teacher at Plumpot Primary School. Most of the other teachers were so old that they talked about the Age of the Dinosaurs as if they had been born then. In fact Dylan, who was nine, was pretty sure that some of the teachers really were dinosaurs. It was just that they hadn't quite fossilized yet, although they seemed well on the way.

Dylan was lucky enough to be in Miss Comet's

class, along with his friends Amy, Lewis and Freya. It was the last day of term and their teacher had just announced that the school was going to play a special Christmas game and the children were impatient to hear what it was.

'Each class is going to research something special to do with Christmas,' smiled Miss Comet, 'and we are going to test Christmas food!'

'Oh wow! I have just died and gone to heaven,' breathed Lewis, who was, to say the least, a large child.

Miss Comet beamed at him and went on, 'We are going to try out some Christmas puddings, to see which ones we like best, and so on.'

Twenty-four children congratulated each other. Four children groaned and gazed at one another as if they had just been sentenced to death, including Lewis, who had decided on the spot that he must be the unluckiest child on Earth. Miss Comet noticed at once, because that's the kind of teacher she was.

'Whatever is the matter with you four?'
Freya's face was pale. 'Please, I don't like
Christmas pudding.'

'And I hate it!' Lewis burst out.
He began making choking noises
and pretended to be sick. Miss
Comet said that she had
got the idea and he
didn't need to perform
a three-act drama about
such a
small thing.
'Anyhow, Lewis, I
thought you liked *all* food?'

'I like everything, miss, everything except Christmas pudding.'

'Christmas pudding stinks!' blurted Amy. 'It's all sticky and yucky and dark.'

'Oh dear,' sighed Miss Comet, turning to Dylan. 'How about you, Dylan? Do you like Christmas pudding?'

Dylan shook his head and gazed sadly at his teacher. 'I'm allergic to it,' he announced flatly.

'Really?'

'Yes. If I eat just the tiniest bit of it I get spots all over and I start shaking and can't stop and I shake and shake until I fall to bits,' Dylan went

on, his imagination going into super-drive. 'My legs and arms fall off, and my head and my ears and nose and everything, even my eyebrows.'

'Goodness me,' cried Miss Comet, wide-eyed. 'We shall need a bucket for all your bits. We certainly can't have that. Very well, you four are excused the tasting. You can write down the pudding scores, all right?'

The four friends nodded seriously and Miss Comet smiled at them encouragingly. She was very understanding, they thought. What they didn't know was that Miss Comet couldn't stand Christmas puddings either and she had no intention of eating any herself.

And the truth of the matter was that soon, the fact that none of them liked Christmas pudding was going to become VERY IMPORTANT INDEED. In fact, Dylan, Freya, Amy, Lewis and Miss Comet were going to have to SAVE THE WORLD!

Ba – ba – ba – ba – BOOOOM!

TWO:
MEANWHILE AT THE
EDGE OF THE UNIVERSE . . .

Here is something shocking that very few people know – Father Christmas has a big brother. Oh yes. His name is Bad Christmas and he is EVIL.

Look at those glinting, piggy eyes. See the
sinister grin twisting his mouth like a snag of
barbed wire. Look at those grabby hands with fat
sausage fingers. Look at that funny little tartan
beanie monkey he's sucking.

WHAT? HE SUCKS A TARTAN BEANIE
MONKEY?

Yes, and the monkey's name is Boo-Boo. Bad
Christmas has had Boo-Boo since he was three.
But don't be fooled – Bad Christmas is so evil that
if you cut out his heart it would probably have
the word EVIL written on it in blood-red letters.
That's assuming you could actually find his heart,
because he probably HASN'T EVEN GOT
ONE!

Bad Christmas does not live in our universe.
He comes from The Other Side, a universe in the
fifth dimension. Yes, Bad Christmas is the monster
behind the Invasion of the Christmas Puddings.
For hundreds of years Bad Christmas has been
imprisoned in this other dimension, for all his

crimes against Christmas. Now he has found a way back into our world, and he has brought his deadly puddings with him. And they are made of STICKY MATTER!

STICKY MATTER? AAAAAARRRGH!

 Our scientific adviser, Professor Damp-Trumpett, explains:

'Oh, PLEEEASE, this is so squeezy-peasy-teasy! Every astro-scientist knows that most of the universe is made of Dark Matter. It is called Dark Matter because you can't actually see it. You might ask, if you can't see it does it matter? In fact, you might even like to call it Does It Matter Matter. Ha ha ha! That's the sort of joke we scientists find very funny indeed. (But nobody else does.) Now then, Bad Christmas has created a new kind of matter to make things from. It is called Sticky Matter and naturally it's very sticky. It is made from sultanas, raisins, peel, flour, nutmeg, eggs, molasses and so on. These things are harmless on their own, but when mixed together they make a foul and stinking sticky goo. It clings to everything. It slithers and oozes and splip-splap-splops. Bad Christmas discovered that if he smeared Sticky Matter along the edge of his universe it would gradually dribble over into our universe! The next thing to do was to find some way to hide himself in enough Sticky Matter to allow himself to slip into our universe too. And so he built a universe-hopping space machine – THE *DEATH PUDDING*!'

Sound FX: Terrible screams echo through space:
'No! Save us! Save us from the *Death Pudding*!'

The *Death Pudding* is a gigantic, slowly revolving
Christmas pudding. Engulfed in flames, it spins
through Deep Space. This is home for Bad
Christmas, a home as big as a football stadium.
This is where he plots and plans. He is going
to take over the world. But first of all he has to
exterminate his brother and take his place.

Yes! He is going to DESTROY FATHER
CHRISTMAS!

TWO AND A HALF: MEANWHILE SOMEWHERE NEAR THE NORTH POLE . . .

Father Christmas stood beside his new rocket-sleigh, whistling 'Jingle Bells' and filling the spaceship's tank from a fuel pump. He gave a cheerful sigh. This was so much easier than feeding reindeer with endless bales of hay.

Mrs Christmas came bustling out of Christmas House. 'I've made you some sandwiches. Are you loaded yet?'

'All done and ready to rocket.' Father Christmas gazed lovingly at his new machine. He was looking forward to this. 'Have you done my sandwiches?'

'Are you deaf? What did I just tell you? What kind of brainless noodle do you think I am?'

'If I'm deaf it's because you shout all the time,'

Father Christmas told her, 'and if you ask me that makes you the biggest brainless noodle in Brainless Noodle-Land.'

'Well, I'm not asking you!' grunted Mrs Christmas. 'I'd rather ask a peanut!'

Father Christmas clapped a hand to his head in mock horror. 'I've got a wife who asks peanuts for advice. You should be on television. They'd call you THE WOMAN WHO TALKS TO PEANUTS.'

Mrs Christmas pursed her lips. Her eyebrows came crashing together in a furious frown. She stamped up to her husband, lifted her chin and glowered at him. There was a moment of frosty staring and then they burst out laughing.

'I talk to peanuts!' chuckled Mrs Christmas, doubling up and slapping her knees. She gently tugged her husband's flowing beard. 'Hello, little peanut. How are you today?' The pair hugged each other hard to stop themselves falling over from too much laughter. Even  the reindeer were giving them strange looks.

At last they stopped. Father Christmas climbed into the rocket-sleigh and strapped himself in. He gazed down fondly at his wife, gave her a wave, pressed a big red button and –

VRRRRRRRROOOOOOSSH!!

The rocket-sleigh shot into the sky. The launch blast tumbled Mrs Christmas into the snow. She lay on her back, legs in the air, while her ball of wool rolled away and half her cardigan unravelled.

'Take good care, jellybean,' Mrs Christmas shouted at the sky as she sat

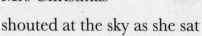

up. 'Come back safely. Now then, where did my needles – ow! I'm sitting on them.'

Far above, the rocket-sleigh was behaving perfectly and Father Christmas tried out some intricate manoeuvres. 'Jingle bells, Batman smells,' he sang cheerfully as he flew along. 'What a fantastic view! I love it up here. These stars must be the best Christmas lights anywhere. They are so . . . oh! What's going on?'

A shiver ran down his spine as Father Christmas watched a strange shadow passing among the stars, blotting them out one by one. At the same time thousands of dark, round objects began to whizz past the spacecraft. They travelled at such speed Father Christmas couldn't make out what they were. It was all rather eerie and he was suddenly filled with a terrible sense of foreboding. Maybe it had something to do with the smell.

'Hmmm, very odd,' he muttered, sniffing the air. 'It smells just like Christmas puddings, and outer space isn't supposed to smell of anything.'

He shuddered. 'How peculiar,' he murmured.
Then he saw it, coming straight for him – a giant
ball of blue flame. It seemed as big as a planet
and beneath the flaming exterior it was awesome,
sinister and very, VERY DARK. It was – the
DEATH PUDDING!

Doo-doo-doo-doo-DOOOOM!

Father Christmas flung the rocket-sleigh into a
handbrake turn and accelerated hard but it was
useless. The *Death Pudding* had caught the little
sleigh in its extra-sticky Sticky Matter traction
beam and was relentlessly reeling in the rocket.

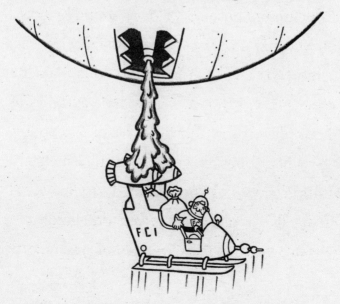

A gaping mouth appeared among the flames on the surface of the *Death Pudding* as the rocket was sucked inside. As the mouth began to close back down Father Christmas, peering fearfully from his sleigh, saw what he had most feared all his life – his big, bad brother!

In his final moments before the mouth shut forever Father Christmas frantically sent out a despairing radio message to his wife.

TWO AND THREE-QUARTERS: AT MUCH THE SAME TIME, IN BRITAIN . . .

Dylan was in a bad mood because that morning he had forgotten his packed lunch for school. His father had told him, as he did every morning, to put it in his school bag.

'Yeah, yeah,' Dylan had muttered. Why did Dad have to say the same thing every day? It was one long checklist. Have you got this, Dylan? Have you got that? Have you got your bag, Dylan? Have you got your brain?

HAVE YOU GOT A LIFE, DAD?!!

That's what

Dylan felt like saying. But he didn't, because Dad was all he had, and when Dylan got cross with Dad he often felt even crosser with himself. Dad was only doing his best, just as he had done since Mum had died. Dad looked after him on his own now, and he didn't do things the way Mum did. He couldn't draw and paint like Mum and he made DREADFUL DISASTER sandwiches – BUT – Dylan loved his dad for trying.

Now Dylan was at school and he had forgotten his horrible sandwiches. Dad would be upset and tell him it was a waste of good food. Dylan would like to tell Dad that a sandwich made of lettuce and chocolate spread was

not exactly 'good food', not even when Dad added ketchup as an extra treat.

Dylan moodily eyed the drawing

of a Christmas pudding he
was doing for the class
project. It didn't look
much like a Christmas
pudding. It looked a
lot more like a fiery
explosion, which was
not surprising because

Dylan had also drawn two enemy aircraft flying
overhead, dropping bombs on the pudding and
blowing it to kingdom come. That's how much he
hated Christmas pudding.

His thoughts were broken by knocking on the
classroom door. Everyone turned to stare. Visitors
to the classroom were rare and nearly always
welcome. However, Dylan was not very impressed
with this one.

'It's your dad!' Amy told him, in case Dylan
couldn't recognize his own father.

It was the first time Miss Comet had met
Dylan's dad, Rufus. He looked flustered as he

explained his mission. 'Dylan forgot his lunch.'

'Oh,' said Miss Comet, and the children sniggered. Dylan's disaster sandwiches were a legend in class.

'Bad luck, Dylan,' murmured Lewis. 'You've got poo-sandwiches after all.'

The class giggled again. Dylan hoped his father hadn't heard Lewis because, even if Lewis was right, it wasn't nice to say.

'He left them in the kitchen,' Rufus mumbled, not taking his eyes off Miss Comet.

'We all get a bit forgetful from time to time,' said Miss Comet, with her lovely smile. 'Do you make Dylan's sandwiches for him?' Dylan's father nodded and Miss Comet continued. 'It's good for the children to have some variety in their lunch. I think Dylan gets a bit bored with lettuce and chocolate spread. Perhaps you could . . .' Miss Comet faltered and blushed. 'Of course, it's not any of my business.'

'No,' blurted Rufus. 'It's fine, really. Variety?

You mean I could change things a bit?'

'Exactly,' laughed Miss Comet.

'I could put the chocolate spread on top of
the lettuce, instead of the lettuce on top of the
chocolate spread?'

Dylan groaned and buried his head in his
hands. Miss Comet swallowed a chuckle. 'It's
not quite what I had in mind. I meant you could
change the fillings. Perhaps you could try cheese
and tomato, or maybe chicken and mayonnaise.'

Rufus's eyes lit up. 'I don't know why I didn't
think of that myself.'

'You've had other things on your mind,' Miss
Comet suggested. 'Looking after a boy of nine all
on your own isn't easy.'

'No.'

'But he's a lovely boy,' Miss Comet went on.

Dylan buried his beetroot face even deeper.

'Come and see what he's doing. Dylan, show
your father your Christmas pudding picture.
There's no need to hide it like that. Sit up and let

us see. Oh! Oh my! Dylan's Christmas pudding seems to be under attack.'

Rufus cleared his throat. 'Dylan doesn't like Christmas pudding. It runs in the family. None of us do. Did. Do.' He was flustered again.

'No, I can see that.' Miss Comet went on to tell Rufus about their project. 'We're going to start taste-testing the puddings this afternoon. At least most of us are. Dylan and a few others will do something else.' She leaned towards Rufus and whispered, 'Can't say I blame them. Christmas puddings are not one of my favourites either.'

'Really?' Rufus smiled for the first time.

'You should do that more often,' said Miss Comet.

'What?'

'Smile.'

'Oh!' The smile vanished and Rufus retreated to the door. 'Best get back to work.'

'And the same goes for us,' nodded Miss Comet. 'Don't forget now – chicken and mayonnaise. I shall be checking.'

'Right,' said Rufus, managing a small grin. 'I'd better watch my step. I wouldn't want to get into trouble with teacher.'

'We'll see about that,' Miss Comet answered, and they gazed at each other for a long time before Dylan's father finally shut the door. He peered back at Miss Comet through the glass for a moment and then vanished.

Dylan let out a sigh. What was *that* all about? Dad had been so edgy. Freya was grinning at him from across the table. 'What?' he asked. 'What now?'

Freya shook her head. 'Boys are so dumb,' she answered and went on with her work, leaving Dylan none the wiser.

THREE:
ON THE
DEATH PUDDING . . .

The moment Father Christmas's rocket-sleigh was inside the *Death Pudding* it was surrounded by dozens of well-armed elves. These were Bad Christmas's 'little helpers', in other words, his army. However, they were strangely dressed for an army, with costumes that made them look

like Boo-Boo – tartan jumpsuits and monkey masks. They were armed to the teeth with Sticky Matter Blatter-Splatters and trained to make an atrociously nasty mess.

 Our on-board scientific expert, Professor Plunk-Grumplett, explains:

'Oh, do come on, this is so simple! The Blatter-Splatter fires a stream of Sticky Matter at high speed. The Sticky Matter sticks to just about anything it touches. (You remember of course that sticky matter is basically Christmas pudding mix.) Anything hit by Sticky Matter is instantly zombified. Now, stop pestering me with silly questions. I'm not a teacher. *I'm* a professor.'

Father Christmas was pulled from his machine,

tied up, tipped on to his side and then rolled like
a barrel before his wicked brother.

'Ho ho ho!' chuckled Bad Christmas with
icy irony. 'Look what we have here! Greetings,
dearest, darling brother. Long time no see!'

'Long time don't want to see – that would be
more like it,' grunted Father Christmas. 'Still
sucking Boo-Boo, I see.'

'Oh dear,' snarled Bad Christmas, stroking
Boo-Boo. 'You *are* in a mood, aren't you? Doesn't
that make a change? Oh yes, indeed. How well
I remember our childhood, so many years ago.

You were always the horribly cheerful one. How everybody loved you!'

Bad Christmas began to prance round the room, pulling faces and talking in a high, copycat voice. 'Look at darling Chrissy-wissy, doesn't he have such lovely podgy red cheeky-weekys? Don't you think his giggle is like eeny-weeny-teeny silver bells!'

Bad Christmas suddenly exploded, his voice dripping hatred. 'You nauseate me, you fat, happy-pappy-dappy doo-dah! But there's nobody to admire you here, little brother. There's no Mummy or Daddy Christmas now, there's just you and me, together again, at last! Plus, of

course, Boo-Boo's army.'
Bad Christmas held the little beanie to his face. 'You're Commander-in-Chief, aren't you, Boo-Boo? Oh yes you are! Clever little monkey!' His eyes flicked back to his brother.

'Welcome to my *Death Pudding*. This fabulous, glorious instrument of doom will be the last thing you'll ever see. What do you think of that?'

'You've always been a crazy maniac,' snorted Father Christmas. 'You haven't changed one bit. You weren't shut away on The Other Side for no reason. You were put there because you were a threat to Christmas throughout the world.'

Bad Christmas thundered across to his brother. 'Oh, listen to Mr Goody-goody! You always were a pompous, self-righteous little toad.' Bad Christmas put one foot on the tubby barrel of rope and began to roll his brother round and round. 'Ha! But look at you now, all tied up and nowhere to go. You'd better face it, little brother, soon you will be nothing but Sticky Matter. I shall turn you into the gloopiest Christmas pudding ever, and it will give me such pleasure. But first I want you to see what is going to happen to all your little friends on Earth.'

Father Christmas turned pale. He knew his big brother was evil and hated him, but he had not realized that Bad Christmas was, well, THAT bad.

'What are you going to do?'

Bad Christmas smiled. Now then, there are different types of smile. When Miss Comet smiles it is as if the sun has just come out from behind a cloud and the world is full of birdsong and blossom and everyone wants to dance, tra-la. When Bad Christmas smiles it is as if the sun has just been

swallowed by a
dense fog of gloom.
Darkness and
Misery stalk the
land; flowers
wilt, birds are
silent and the
only dance is a
dismal trudge.

'Do let me explain, little brother,' said
Bad Christmas. 'In fact, let me give you AN
EXAMPLE!' Bad Christmas turned to his
elves. 'You! Bring me some pudding, and, you
lot – bring me the polar bear.' The way Bad
Christmas's voice changed was truly scary. It was
equally full of scorn and cream. One moment it
would soothe and caress and then it would lash
out like a whip.

The elves scurried away and it wasn't long
before they returned, one with a small Christmas
pudding and several others leading a chained and

muzzled polar bear. The noble animal had been reduced to a starved and shambling wreck. The fear in its eyes would have melted anyone's heart – anyone, that is, except Bad Christmas.

Bad Christmas took the pudding to the bear. 'There, no need to be alarmed. Look, I bring you some lovely food. Aren't you hungry? Doesn't it smell delicious? Oh yes! Do eat some. I know you haven't been fed for days – you must be so awfully hungry. Have a nibble. Yes, feast away to your heart's content.'

The starving bear gulped down the poisonous pudding while Bad Christmas clapped his hands. 'Look, Boo-Boo! No creature can resist our Christmas puddings. Now, do watch closely and observe what happens next.'

The bear began to shake its head from side to side, as if thousands of bees were inside its ears and it was trying to shake them out. Suddenly it went rigid, standing on tiptoe. Its eyes bulged, a strange light flaring up in them before quickly fading away to nothing at all. The bear's body went limp and it stood there, still and silent as a statue.

'Take off the chains and muzzle,' commanded Bad Christmas. He looked at the bear and said, 'Mr Boo-Boo says come here.' The bear shambled forward with oddly mechanical steps. 'Boo-Boo says lift your right paw. Lift your left paw. Pick your nose. Pat your bottom.'

With each command Bad Christmas gave a silly giggle as the bear obeyed. The bear's mind was entirely under his control. Not only that, but Bad Christmas didn't even have to speak the commands – he merely had to *think* them and the animal obeyed. It was terrifying that anyone could have such power, but Father Christmas had no idea how it would help his brother take over the world.

'It's simple, dear little-brained brother,' explained Bad Christmas. 'I have an endless supply of puddings. They have invaded Earth and are sitting innocently on every shop and supermarket shelf around the globe. Many have already been bought. On Christmas Day millions of people will be tucking into MY Christmas puddings, which are made with Sticky Matter, and then what happened to the polar bear will happen to them. Just

Ho ho ho ho ho!

the teeniest taste and they will be MY SLAVES! My puddings will turn everyone into zombies. Ho ho ho ho ho! Ho ho ho ho!'

Sound FX: Screams of horror from a distant Earth, and heavy, doom-laden music. Dooooo-dee-dooooooom! Booooo bee-booooom!

Bad Christmas's laughter echoed throughout the *Death Pudding* and his elves joined in with their own horrible ho-ho chorus.

'STOP!' Bad Christmas roared, glowering at everyone. Several elves fell over from the sheer force of his bellow, while others scuttled to the far edges of the room and shrank back against the walls. Bad Christmas stalked across to his brother.

'DARLING brother,' he purred. 'Maybe you are wondering why I am doing this. Do let me enlighten you. All my life I have hated you. You know why? Because you are loved by everyone you meet. Even when I was a toddler and you were a tiny baby if anyone saw you they went all cootchy-coo and isn't he cute and – urrrrrgh!'

Bad Christmas shuddered at the memory. 'And when the time came for one of us to take over from Father, WHO was chosen? Surely it would be ME? The ELDEST? But, no. Everyone said I would scare the children. Imagine – little old me scaring the tiddly tiny-tots? Oh dear, can't have that – oh no! AND THEY CHOSE YOU INSTEAD!

'You take presents round year after year and they all love you so much. It makes me SICK! Do you think I got presents on The Other Side? Of course not. Did anyone remember me? No. Well, I am going to change all that. This year there will only be one person getting presents and that person is going to be ME! Everyone will bow before me and bring ME gifts. It will be the best Christmas ever.'

'You can't make people give you presents,' said Father Christmas. 'A present is something someone wants to give you. That's the whole point.'

'Oh, Boo-Boo, did you hear prissy-pants? Of course I can make them. I am going to turn everyone into a pudding-zombie and then they will do exactly what I say. And I shall start with the children. I have made some extra-special tiny puddings, covered in lovely crunchy chocolate. One tiny bite and they'll be in my control forever. And here's the best bit. Who do you think is going to give the children their special choccy Chrissy puds? Father Christmas himself! *You* are going to put one of my special puds in every child's Christmas stocking. So if anyone ever discovers the deadly secret of the pudding, they'll think it was YOU! Oh, Boo-Boo, isn't that hilarious?!'

'You'll never be able to make me do that!' groaned Father Christmas.

'Yes, I will,' hissed his monstrous big brother. 'You will soon obey all my commands. Elves! Take Father Christmas to the Pudding Laboratory and prepare him for zombification!'

49

Father Christmas struggled and squirmed, but it was pointless. His efforts only made Bad Christmas laugh even louder, while his elf army rolled his younger brother out of the chamber and towards the grisly lab.

Sound and lighting FX: Huge noise of thunderstorm, lightning flashes and wailing voices of doom. Manic monkey-type voice squeals: 'They're all going to die! Ha ha ha ha ha!'

THREE AND A LITTLE HALF: MEANWHILE AT THE NORTH POLE . . .

BAD CHRISTMAS. That is all the message said – only those two words had come through the crackling radio from outer space. Mrs Christmas wrote them down and now she read them again and again. 'Oh dear, oh dear. What am I supposed to do?'

She knew all about Bad Christmas. There were umpteen family stories that Father Christmas had told her about his wicked, older brother. There was the time he had strapped rockets to their mother's armchair while she was asleep in it in an attempt to blast her into outer space. Luckily the chair only shot from the house as far as the barn, where it buried itself in a mound of straw.

There was the time he was supposed to feed the

reindeer and Bad Christmas gave them nothing but baked beans to eat. When Father Christmas took to the skies he was overcome by ghastly gases. He fainted, fell out and almost plunged to his death. He was only saved because his big red robe ballooned up like a parachute.

Now Mrs Christmas was facing a terrifying problem. She had no idea where her husband was, nor what had happened to him. All she knew was that Bad Christmas had returned and her husband must be in deadly trouble. She wandered the house, thinking and knitting very hard. She even spoke to the reindeer about it, though they couldn't answer.

Strangely enough, it was the reindeer that gave her an idea. Maybe she didn't know where Father Christmas was, but that would not stop her looking for him. She had the old sleigh and the reindeer. They could track him down!

Mrs Christmas threw several bales of hay into the sleigh for the reindeer, along with a fur blanket, sandwiches and a flask of tea for herself. The reindeer were already frisky. They were pretty bored with having nothing to do. Now they could hardly wait.

Mrs Christmas harnessed them to the sleigh, climbed on board and with a swoosh and a swish they took to the skies. 'Fly, my beauties!' cried Mrs Christmas. 'Seek out your master, wherever he is! Fly as fast as you can!'

These were brave words because the truth was that Mrs Christmas had never had a reindeer driving lesson in her life. She seemed to think that all she had to do was shout 'Fly!' and they would. The reindeer did take off, but unfortunately she forgot to give them any idea of what direction they should go. Some went left and others turned right. Some went up and others went down.

The result was that the sleigh carved great loops in the sky. It performed several unintended barrel-rolls. It swooped, swerved, zigged and zagged as if every single reindeer had been given a different map. She was last seen powering straight upwards in a terrifying death climb. Back on Earth a faint cry for help drifted down from the dark sky. What goes up must come down, as everyone knows. But where?

THREE AND RATHER A BIT MORE THAN A HALF: AND AT PLUMPOT PRIMARY . . .

Twenty-four children, each armed with a spoon, sat round several Christmas puddings. Little did they know that although the puddings had been bought off the supermarket shelf they had in fact come from The Other Side.

Dylan held his nose. 'Anyone got a sick-bucket?'

'Dylan, just because you don't like Christmas pudding there's no need to make a fuss,' Miss Comet pointed out. 'You four watch the others and see if you can tell which pudding they will choose as the best one.'

'There can't be a best

one, miss,' said Freya. 'All Christmas puddings are horrible, so they'll have to choose the worst one.'

'Very funny, Freya,' said Miss Comet. 'You're worse than Dylan. All right, the rest of you, tuck in and test them out.'

Twenty-four spoons dug away at the puddings. The children's jaws began to move more and more slowly. Silence descended. One girl began to shake her head, as if a thousand bees were inside and she was trying to shake them out. Another did the same, and another. Then, like a ballet-chorus, they all rose together on tiptoe. Their eyes lit up and then the flame quickly faded. Their bodies went limp and still. The classroom was filled with an eerie silence.

Miss Comet's eyes whizzed from one child to the next. Surely there must be signs of life somewhere? But all was deathly still. Miss Comet ran to the nearest child.

'Abbie? What's up? Talk to me!' She shook Abbie, but the girl just gazed glassily ahead and made no sound or movement of her own. Miss Comet tried Liam, but he was the same and so were the others.

Dylan, Amy, Lewis and Freya watched with alarm as Miss Comet raced from one zombified child to another. It was Freya who pointed the finger of blame.

'It was those Christmas puddings, miss.'

The four children and their teacher looked at each other, speechless.

Then, as they stood there a weird thing happened. The twenty-four zombies pushed back their chairs in unison. They stood up. They lifted their right arms and then their left. They picked their noses, patted their bottoms and finally they sat down.

Miss Comet was now mega-gobsmacked. What

was that all about? (Of course, she had no idea that at that same moment, out in Deep Space, Bad Christmas was experimenting with the polar bear. Since Miss Comet's children were also now under his control they had to obey his orders too.)

Dylan went to the nearest table, picked up one of the puddings and began to examine it.

'Drop that at once!' yelled Miss Comet with alarm, racing across the room and sending the pudding crashing to the floor. 'Wash your hands straight away!'

'I was only looking,' began the astonished Dylan. His teacher had never shouted like that before.

'Sorry, but we have no idea what's going on here. Those puddings could be dangerous and I don't want any more of you to go . . . like them. Oh dear, poor things. What will their parents say?'

Freya gave a snort. 'I should think Tricia's mum will be pretty pleased. She's always telling Tricia to stop mucking about and bumping into things. Tricia's mum says she's worse than an elephant in an egg box.'

'Freya, I know Tricia can be a bit boisterous but even so I'm sure her mother will be very upset. Amy and Lewis, go and ask the head teacher to come here at once. It's an emergency. Go on, and you can run in the corridor. Run like the wind!'

Miss Comet turned back to the class. They hadn't budged a single centimetre and were still staring lifelessly straight ahead. Dylan and Freya moved closer to their teacher, where they felt a bit safer. This was getting a bit too creepy. Freya tried to hold Dylan's hand.

'Gerroff,' he growled, pulling away and folding his arms across his chest. Miss Comet bit back a tiny smile and held Freya's hand herself.

'They look like puppets,' Freya whispered.

Mr Dingle, the head teacher, hurried in, closely followed by Lewis and Amy. As Miss Comet told him what had happened Mr Dingle checked each child. He got out his mobile and phoned for medical and police help. He couldn't explain what had taken place any more than the others, but he could see it was serious.

From that moment on everything seemed to get taken away from Miss Comet and the children. At least, that was how it felt to them. The police came with a medical team. They had to answer lots of questions and although the Christmas puddings were mentioned the police said they reckoned it was a gas leak.

'I can smell gas,' insisted

the inspector. Dylan said he suspected Warren.

'He's always letting off,' said Dylan.

'Yeah,' agreed Lewis. 'He's positively volcanic at times.'

But the inspector only told them not to be rude. Lewis and Dylan looked at each other. Rude? They were reporting a known fact about Warren. But they could tell from the inspector's face that there was no point in saying anything more. The inspector called the gas services and the classroom was cordoned off. It was all so noisy, what with people shouting and rushing about, sirens coming and going, and tape being thrown around the classroom.

Miss Comet and the four children got pushed further and further away.

'It's not gas,' whispered Amy, as if she was afraid she might be arrested for disagreeing with the inspector. 'It was those Christmas puddings.'

'I know, Amy,' nodded Miss Comet. 'I don't like this at all. We must do something about it. But what *can* we do?'

'Well,' began Dylan, 'I reckon someone
poisoned the puddings. I always thought
Christmas puddings were horrible.'

'You might be right,' said Miss Comet. 'But why
would anyone want to turn children into –' she
broke off, unsure how to describe them.

'Zombies,' said Lewis. 'They're
zombies, like in that film,
Zombie Monster Terror. All these
zombies attack a town and
they start eating everyone
and you see this man's eyeball
popping out and a zombie eats it
and –'

'Yes, thank you, Lewis. That's
quite enough. You shouldn't be
watching films like that. It's not nice. But yes,
they are like zombies, and the way they all did
the same thing at the same time – it was as if
someone had control of them. Why would anyone

want to control them like that?'

'Perhaps they want to be a teacher, miss,' said Freya, and Miss Comet gave a weak sigh.

'Freya, it's when you make remarks like that that I wish I could control you, but I do realize that's impossible. Now then, we can't just stand here doing nothing but where do we start?'

At that moment there was a strange whooshing noise from high above and a moment later a dreadful – *KER-BANNG KERR-RANNGLE SPING-DING-DANG KERLATTERLY KRRRASH!*

A sleigh pulled by six reindeer had made a mad attempt to land on the roof of the school hall. Mrs Christmas overshot wildly and the reindeer went plunging over the edge. Now they were dangling in mid-air, while the sledge itself was teetering on the edge, about to fall at any moment.

Mrs Christmas shouted 'Whoa' and 'Stop!' several seconds too late and then waved at everyone. 'Hello!' she shouted, getting to her feet. It was the worst thing to do. The sleigh slid forward a few more centimetres and then toppled over the edge. Down it fell – SLUMP!! – and soon there was a great complication of reindeer, sledge and Mrs Christmas, all legs, arms and heads wriggling and groaning on the ground.

FOUR:
DEEP INSIDE THE
DEATH PUDDING . . .

Father Christmas was not happy. The tartan
monkey-elves had released him, but only so they
could strap him to the big operating table in the
laboratory. Unable to move, Father Christmas
anxiously glanced round the room.

The circular walls were lined with row upon
row of cages of all sizes. Almost every one
was occupied. There were monkeys and mice,
rabbits and ravens, tigers, terrapins and tizzwots.
(Tizzwots come from another solar system. They
have six legs, are very pretty and like eating
chocolate biscuits.)

There must have been at least a hundred
different animals locked away in the laboratory,
including the polar bear, and most had that

same lifeless look in their eyes. They had been puddified.

Next to the operating table stood a large tank. Father Christmas could feel the heat it gave off, and an unmistakable smell of Christmas pudding hung in the air. A large steel pipe poked out from near the bottom of the tank. It fed into a glass container which also had a piston in it, slowly pumping up and down.

From there a glass tube travelled upwards. When it reached the ceiling it turned at a right angle and crossed to a position directly above the table, where it fed into a large funnel. The funnel ended in a short section of floppy, red rubber tubing. Father Christmas had a very uneasy feeling in the pit of his stomach.

A warning siren went off and the elves hurried to the sides of the room, standing to attention as Bad Christmas made a triumphant entrance.

'This is a moment I have dreamed about,' he crooned. 'And now here you are, all tucked up in bed and ready for a nightcap. Boo-Boo says open your mouth like a good boy. I do hope you're ready for my wonderful machine.'

Father Christmas watched with alarm as the monstrous engine above his head began to move slowly towards him. 'What is this infernal machine?'

'A little toy of mine. It's my Megamatic-Sticky-Matter-Injectatomic-Pump, but I usually call it The Puddifier.'

Here is our science expert explanationist, Professor Dank-Bumpott:

'Haven't any of you got brains of your own? Surely you know what a Megamatic-Sticky-Matter-Injectatomic-Pump does? It forces the Sticky Matter, perhaps better known as Christmas pudding, into any receptacle placed underneath the funnel. The machine can be used to fill a bowl, cake tin, bath, swimming pool, even a ship. In this case of course the receptacle will be Father Christmas's mouth.'

Sound FX: Giant clash of cymbals. Oh no! Bad Christmas is going to puddify Father Christmas!

'You'll never get me to eat that poisonous gloop of yours,' growled Father Christmas through gritted teeth.

69

'Oh, good! Look, Boo-Boo, he's going to struggle! Just what I wanted. Now I shall have to force it down you. Switch on The Puddifier!'

Steam hissed. Nasty smells spilled from the tank. The piston in the glass chamber pumped up and down. A series of muffled burps came from deep within the tank. Father Christmas watched with horror as a line of dark brown mini-puds entered the glass chamber. Centimetre by centimetre the puddings made their way upwards until they dropped one by one into the funnel. The rubber tubing bulged as the puddings edged closer and closer to Father Christmas's mouth.

Bands of steel held his head tight. The first pudding was slowly squeezed from the rubber tube. Out it came, SPLOP! But Father Christmas kept his mouth firmly shut and the pudding bounced harmlessly off his chin.

Amazingly, instead of being furious, Bad Christmas rubbed his hands with glee. 'Boo-Boo, it's going just as we planned. Now we come to the best bit. This is what I've been waiting for. Watch this, everyone.'

As a second pudding began to emerge from the rubber tube, Bad Christmas leaned across the table and with two fingers held Father Christmas's nose tight shut. The poor man struggled to breathe and at last he had to open his mouth, just as the next pudding tumbled out and – SPLOP! It vanished down his throat.

It was over. All the clamps were released. 'There,' said Bad Christmas soothingly. 'Didn't that taste nice?'

Father Christmas shook his head as if his ears were filled with bees. He was released from the table. His eyes dull and lifeless, he stood still, totally zombified.

'Now then, dear brother, my elves will show you to your new home. It's such a lovely cage. I'm sure you'll like it. You will remain here until Christmas Eve and then you are going to take your sleigh, loaded down with my chocolate-covered puddings, and you are going to give one to every child in the land. Oh ho ho, I can't wait!'

Oh no! Bad Christmas is setting up his brother as a master criminal!

FOUR AND
THE REST OF IT: 🌍
BACK ON EARTH . . .

The police had declared Plumpot Primary School
a disaster zone, what with a major reindeer pile-
up, twenty-four puddified children and Warren's
supposed gas leak. A fleet of ambulances waited
beside Miss Comet's classroom. The zombified
children were taken on board and whisked off to
hospital for examination. It wouldn't do any good.
Doctors would be totally baffled but wouldn't
admit it. Instead they would almost certainly
announce that it was 'a virus'.

Miss Comet and the four children told the
police again and again that Christmas puddings
were the key to the whole business. The inspector
in charge listened wearily.

'I blame television,' he grumbled. 'There are

so many police dramas these days that everyone thinks they're a detective and can solve mysteries. It's not like that in real life. We hardly ever solve anything.' He sighed. 'All right, we'll send off some Christmas pudding for examination.'

'How long will that take?' asked Miss Comet.

'Four weeks,' the inspector told her.

'We can't wait four weeks! It's almost Christmas Day! Don't you understand?'

'All right, miss, I think you've taken up enough of our time.'

'But you have to do something now!' Miss Comet cried.

'No need to get carried away, miss,' said the inspector, rather more forcefully.

'Aren't you even going to attend to the reindeer pile-up?'

'That's for Animal Rescue, miss. We have notified them but they've been delayed by an injured hedgehog. Got a bit flattened apparently and they're trying to plump it up. Now then, you're in the way of my men – move along there.'

'He wouldn't listen, would he?' said Freya, seeing Miss Comet's angry face when she returned. Amy wanted to know what they were going to do.

'Somebody has to help those poor reindeer,' announced Miss Comet firmly. 'Come on. We are going to untangle them.'

They got to work and carefully began to unhook antlers, descramble legs and get the reindeer back on their feet. At the bottom of the pile they discovered a very old lady, rather tubby and badly dressed in a woolly cardigan that appeared to be coming undone at all its edges, a thick skirt and striped woolly stockings.

'What a business! Did you know reindeer don't have brakes? Well, they don't but they jolly well should. Goodness knows how Father Christmas managed to stop them. Can you see my knitting needles anywhere? Oh, thank you.'

Lewis was staring at the old woman and at last he blurted out the question

burning his tongue. 'Are you Father Christmas's wife?'

'Yes, I am, though sometimes I wonder why, daft old bag that he is. Now then, what's going on here? What are those flashing lights for, and the amblydance, the ambi-thing – you know! What's it all about?'

Miss Comet filled in the details. Mrs Christmas couldn't believe her ears. Her eyes sparkled and she almost danced. 'It's all beginning to make sense!'

'It is?' asked Miss Comet. 'Thank goodness!'

'Don't get too excited, dear. I don't know everything and I certainly don't know what to do. Where shall I start? I have received an urgent message from my husband. It was just two words – BAD CHRISTMAS.'

'What does that mean?' asked Amy.

'Bad Christmas is the name of my husband's brother.'

Dylan snorted. 'Father Christmas doesn't have a brother.'

'My dear child,' said Mrs Christmas patiently, 'I think I'm in a better position than you to know that. You have never heard of him because for the last two hundred years he has been imprisoned on The Other Side. That's how bad he is. He wasn't born bad, but when he was three he was given Christmas pudding to eat. He didn't like it and spat it out. His parents made him eat it and he hated it. He never forgave them. He's had a thing about Christmas pudding ever since.

'I think there's a connection between Bad Christmas and the puddings that have zombified your classmates. He is certainly behind this, but what is he trying to do, and why? It's bound to be something horribly evil. For one thing, I am pretty sure that he has captured my husband.'

'Bad Christmas has kidnapped Father Christmas?' asked Lewis. 'Doesn't that mean there won't be any Christmas?'

'It seems like it, but even that may not be Bad Christmas's plan. I think he's got something else up his sleeve.'

At that moment they were interrupted as Dylan's father pushed his way into the little circle.

'Dylan! Thank goodness you're all right! I came as quickly as I could.'

'Dad, OK, you can put me down. Stop hugging me so hard. Daaaad!' Dylan struggled free, red-faced and embarrassed, while Miss Comet watched with an interested smile. Rufus acknowledged her with a nod.

'What's going on?' he asked. As he listened he frowned and his eyes narrowed. 'So we need to find Father Christmas and his brother? Mrs Christmas, you know more about them than anyone – what's the best way to do that?'

'My idea was to let the reindeer sniff out my

husband. The big problem is that I'm no good at handling reindeer.' She glanced back at the accident scene. 'As you saw.'

'I've driven a horse and cart a few times,' Miss Comet offered and a wave of excitement swept through the little group.

'Let's go, then,' cried Mrs Christmas, and they hurried after her.

'I think Miss Comet is brilliant,' Amy whispered to the others.

'So does Dylan's dad,' sniggered Freya, glancing at the pair as they strode along beside each other, talking and smiling.

FIVE:
THREE DAYS
LATER AND IT'S
CHRISTMAS EVE!

Father Christmas worked mechanically, trudging up and down roofs, dropping down chimneys and filling stockings with chocolate-covered puddings. He ignored the mince pies, sweets and drinks that had been left out for him. He didn't notice astonished eyes peeping out from beneath covers. He didn't feel the odd crazy dog tugging at his boots and barking at the world to announce he'd just caught a burglar and wasn't he clever? He just trudged back and forth like a zombie because, of course, he *was* a zombie!

Already, in some houses, children were sneakily opening their stockings. They found their charming little chocolate ball, wrapped up in shiny paper. Chocolate in the middle of the night when you are supposed to be sleeping is the best kind of chocolate there is! They bit into it. They shook their heads. Their eyes glazed over and they collapsed back on their beds, waiting for orders – orders that could only come from Bad Christmas.

The *Death Pudding* was orbiting Earth. In the Command Centre Bad Christmas and his elves kept track of Father Christmas, making sure that everything was going to plan. But why did nobody on Earth spot the *Death Pudding*? After all, the planet is covered with telescopes and radar stations, all pointing their equipment at the sky.

 Our chief scientific adviserator, Professor Bonk-Drumkitt, explains:

 'Now, listen, I'm getting very tired of having to explain things all the time. It must be clear to the smallest brain that nobody could see the

Death Pudding. Why not, you may ask? Because it was invisible. Bad Christmas had covered the *Death Pudding* with a cloak of Invisibility Cream. Invisibility Cream is an ultra-thin special cream made up of millicules. As you may know, all things in the universe are made of molecules. That is, all things *except* Invisibility Cream, which is made from *millicules*. Millicules are the exact opposite of molecules because whereas we know molecules exist, millicules *don't* – that's why they're invisible! I told you it was simple. Now then, if you bother me with one more question I shall put you all in detention. Goodbye!'

The elves in the Command Centre were getting jittery. Some of them had spotted a blip on the radar, something that shouldn't have been there. Big Chief Elf shuffled across to Bad Christmas, who was standing at the great window gazing fondly at the blue planet below and sucking Boo-Boo's right ear.

'Great Master, an unknown object is tracking Father Christmas.'

'Really?' Bad Christmas's eyes narrowed a fraction. 'Hmmmm. I wonder what that could possibly be? A fighter jet from some daft country, maybe?'

'No, Great Master. It is too slow and it wanders around too much.'

'Indeed? How intriguing. Move the *Death Pudding* to a position where we can make contact, if necessary. Prepare to seize it with the tractor beam.'

Big Chief altered course and soon the machine of doom was silently slipping round the Earth.

'And there it is!' cried Bad Christmas. 'Oh, joy of joys! It's Father Christmas's sleigh! That can only be his dear, darling wife, Mrs Christmas. How nice it will be to see her again after all these years. It will be quite a family reunion.'

A scowl descended upon his face. 'Bring the *Death Pudding* closer. Prepare an ambush team and make sure they are well armed with Sticky Matter Blatter-Splatters. I will lead them. I don't want that interfering old bag mucking things up. We must get her. Now, go!'

Bad Christmas turned back to the window and rubbed his hands. 'Oh, goodness me, I'm getting quite excited. Christmas is coming! Ho ho ho ho ho!'

FIVE AND A BIT: AMBUSHED!

'We've been searching for almost three days and we're running out of sandwiches!' wailed Mrs Christmas, tense with frustration. She suddenly stood up in the sleigh and yelled at the top of her voice. 'Jellybean! Where are you, you stupid stocking-stuffer?'

No answer came back from the star-spangled heavens, but the sleigh wobbled alarmingly, and Miss Comet grabbed at Mrs Christmas and pulled her back into the seat.

'I do wish you wouldn't do that. I'm sure we will find him – eventually. At least the reindeer still seem to be on some kind of trail.'

Mrs Christmas grunted. 'Huh. They spent the whole of yesterday just creeping about outer space looking for Christmas puddings, if you remember. They never think of anything except their own stomachs. And heaven alone knows why outer space smelled of Christmas pudding anyway. It's all rather odd, if you ask me.'

Miss Comet smiled to herself. After three days of sitting next to Mrs Christmas she had grown used to the barrage of complaints that came from her. As for herself, Miss Comet had proved to be a dab hand at team driving. She sat at the reins, with a huge fur rug pulled up to her chin and Mrs Christmas beside her, giving helpful comments from time to time as she caught up with her knitting.

'Tuck the bottom edge of the rug right under your feet. You'll find the draught doesn't get up your skirt, dear. I told dear old jellybean he needed something better than this windy antique, but did he listen? No – not until last year when he got back with such a stinking cold his sneezes blew tiles off our roof.'

There was not enough rug for Rufus and the
children to snuggle under and they had to make
do with a pile of old toy sacks, while snow whirled
round them, into their eyes and ears, up their
noses and down their necks. They climbed inside
the sacks, pulling the tops over their heads and lay
huddled together, shivering and grumbling in the
back of the sleigh.

The reindeer galloped the sky, tracking down

their master. It was a complicated task. They lost the scent completely at one point because the strong odour of Christmas pudding was hanging about that particular area. It took the reindeer hours before they eventually managed to pick out the faint whiff of Father Christmas and set off once more.

Once they had picked up a fresh trail they made steady progress, and at last they began to plunge down towards Earth, faster and faster.

'I think they're on to something!' whispered Miss Comet excitedly, and Mrs Christmas immediately stood up to get a better look. 'SIT DOWN, YOU MAD OLD BAT!' squeaked Miss Comet frantically as the sleigh almost turned right over.

Mrs Christmas hastily took her seat and smiled sheepishly while Miss Comet turned bright red and spluttered an apology. 'I'm so sorry. I didn't mean to say that. I was just . . .'

'It's quite all right, dear,' chuckled Mrs

Christmas. 'That's exactly what my husband calls me. Makes me feel quite at home.' She suddenly leaped up from her seat again.

'Look! There it is! There's the rocket-sleigh, right next to those houses!'

Poor Miss Comet saved the sleigh from a major accident yet again and calmly turned to her companion. 'Mrs Christmas, if you do that once more I shall make you sit in the back with the others. There's to be no more bad behaviour.'

The two women exchanged glances and burst out laughing. 'Set down here,' said Mrs Christmas. 'Bad Christmas may be close by. We shall have to creep up carefully.'

Miss Comet brought the sleigh down for a

perfect landing. While the reindeer shook snow from their antlers and steamed quietly from their efforts, she helped Mrs Christmas down.

'You were born to command a sleigh,' Mrs Christmas told her. 'That was quite superb, especially for a first time.'

A muffled noise came from beside them.

'What did you say?' asked Mrs Christmas.

Rufus growled back, 'I said, can we come out yet? Has it stopped snowing? We're freezing!'

'No, stay there and try and keep warm. We're going to see what Father Christmas is doing. We'll be back in a jiffy.'

The women set off across the snow towards the houses. They were almost at the rocket-sleigh when they saw Father Christmas returning from his mission. Mrs Christmas brightened at once.

'There he is, the dear old walrus. He's walking a bit funnily, don't you think? He looks like a robot.' Mrs Christmas was looking around warily. 'There's no sign of his wicked brother anyway.

That's good. Let's go and hear what he has to say for himself. Fancy sending out a message like that when everything seems to be fine. Hey, jellybean! What's up with your legs? You look like one of your mechanical toys. Have your batteries run down?'

Father Christmas ignored her. He collected another sack and began to clump back to the houses. Mrs Christmas hurried up to him and tapped him on his shoulder.

'Don't ignore me, you fat tomato. And look at me when I'm talking to you!' Mrs Christmas tried to stand in front of him, but Father Christmas simply carried on walking. She stumbled back into the snow and he trudged right across her. 'Hey! That's not funny!'

Mrs Christmas struggled to her feet and ran after him. She waved a hand in front of his glassy eyes. She slapped his face and beat her fists on top of his head. 'Listen to me! I'm talking to you, you great clod-poll!'

'Do stop fussing, woman, and let him go. It won't do the slightest bit of good.'

Light and Sound FX: Enormous cymbal clash, accompanied by lightning flashes and huge dark clouds scudding across sky at high speed. *Pish! Fizzz! KRRANNGG! Pish!*

Mrs Christmas spun round and found herself staring aghast at someone she hadn't seen for many, many years.

'Bad Christmas,' she whispered. 'It IS you behind all this! But how did you escape from The Other Side?'

'I'm far cleverer than you think,' Bad Christmas sneered.

Mrs Christmas snorted. 'I see you haven't given up Boo-Boo yet.'

Bad Christmas pretended to claw at Mrs Christmas with the beanie monkey. 'Raargh, raargh!' he growled. 'That's right, Boo-Boo, scratch her eyes out.'

Mrs Christmas turned away in despair.

Raargh, raargh!

'Help!' Miss Comet cried. 'I'm being kidnapped by tartan monkeys!' Several elves were trying to pull Miss Comet in different directions. 'Let me go!'

'My, my, you're a feisty one, aren't you? Don't

bother struggling,' crooned Bad Christmas. 'It won't get you anywhere. If you break free my elves will simply shoot you down with Sticky Matter. Right then, now that I have you two safely in my care, we can leave Father Christmas to get on with his task. We'll go and fetch your ridiculous sleigh. What century do you think we're in, the seventeenth? Huh! Give me a *Death Pudding* every time!'

Bad Christmas turned to Big Chief Elf. 'I shall take the prisoners to the ship. You take four elves and bring the sleigh and reindeer on board. I want everyone to see my moment of triumph when the world brings ME presents and I sit on Father Christmas's throne!'

Sound FX: More thunder, lightning and generally scary stuff.

FIVE AND A LITTLE BIT MORE: THINGS GET EVEN WORSE...

'I'm bored,' muttered Dylan.

Freya giggled from deep inside her sack. 'We could play I-spy.'

'Oh, great,' Lewis groaned. 'I-spy from inside a sack.'

'Ssssh!' hissed Rufus. 'Someone's coming back.'

A faint, rhythmic sound drew closer. 'Left, right, left, right, Ambush Party – halt!'

'That's not them,' whispered Rufus anxiously. 'Whatever happens, keep quiet.'

Big Chief carefully avoided the reindeer. He hated big, four-legged animals. Their front ends had nasty teeth. Their sides had kicky legs and as for their back ends – that was the most dangerous bit of all.

'Ambush Party, climb aboard. You lot sit in the back with those sacks. Go on, get a move on!' The four junior elves climbed over the seat and tumbled on to the sacks.

'Ow!' squeaked Amy. Everyone froze. The children, Rufus, the elves – all of them. At last Big Chief spoke.

'Did you say "ow"?' he asked one of the elves.

'No, Chief.'

'Did you say "ow"?'

'Not me, Chief.'

'You?'

'Very much not at all, Chief. Didn't say nuffink.'

Big Chief's eyes narrowed to suspicious slits. He peered over the front seat at the sacks. 'Give that one there a good kick.'

One of the elves gave Rufus's sack a thumping kick. It got him right in the middle of his back but he had his teeth firmly gritted and didn't make a sound.

'Try that one,' pointed Big Chief, and another

elf gave Amy's sack a cracking whump.

'OW!' yelled Amy.

'Idiot,' hissed Lewis, then clapped a hand to his mouth, but it was too late. The elves were already pulling the two sacks apart and hauling out the children. Amy had tears in her eyes and a bruise on her arm.

'It really hurt, Lewis,' she complained and he grunted an apology.

'Two more prisoners for Bad Christmas!' cried Big Chief. 'He will be pleased.'

'What about these sacks, Chief?' asked one of

the elves.

'Kick 'em.'

Freya and Dylan both received heavy wallops, but they managed to stay quiet. 'That's all there are, Chief,' the elves reported.

'Let's get going, then. I'm starving and I need a smackerel or two. Giddy up, you stupid reindeer! Get on with it!'

SIX:
BAD CHRISTMAS
BECOMES A TV STAR,
SORT OF . . .

Bad Christmas swaggered up and down the
Command Centre deck. He was almost ready for
the greatest moment of his life but first of all he
had a little bit of business with Planet Earth.

'Prepare me for my audience!' he ordered his
elves. 'Where's Make-Up? Come on, get a move
on. I have an adoring public to address. Are the
cameras rolling? Do stop waving that brush in my
face, YOU'RE SCARING BOO-BOO! What do
you mean, he bit you? Serves you right. No, I will
definitely NOT have blue eye make-up. I don't
care if it does make me look soft and gentle. I am
Bad Christmas, Master of Earth, Commander of
Billions and still counting!'

It was sad but true. Bad Christmas was

achieving his dream. Millions of children across the world had eaten their mini chocolate puddings. And those people without children were tucking into their Christmas dinners and guess what was for pudding? Man by man, woman by woman, and child by child they became puddified. Even pets fell beneath Bad Christmas's spell, as their owners fed them little titbits off the festive table. Dogs, cats, rabbits, hamsters, even budgerigars turned into zombies.

Bad Christmas was ready to speak to the world. Television channels round the globe were interrupted as his broadcast went out. Screens flickered for a moment and there was Bad

Christmas. And Boo-Boo.

'Hello, viewers! Yes, it is dearest me, the new Father Christmas, and Boo-Boo here, saying Happy Chewing to all you lovely puddified people. Do give me a cheer, hip hip —'

A robotic cry of 'Hooray!' drifted up from the planet.

'I thank you, I thank you,' drooled Bad Christmas, getting up, giving a bow and strutting up and down.

'Sit down, or you go off camera,' warned TV Director Elf as the two cameras tried to keep track of the wandering megalomaniac. Bad Christmas stopped in his tracks.

'Don't you tell me what to do!' he snapped back. 'I am Supreme Commander of All Things and I'll do what I like.'

'Yes, but you'll still go off camera if you stand up,' insisted TV Director Elf.

'I'll speak to you later,' hissed Bad Christmas.

'Raargh! Raargh!' went Boo-Boo.

TV Director Elf's lower lip wobbled a moment and he threw down his clipboard. 'Right, that's it! I will not be threatened by a beanie monkey or told how to make a TV broadcast. This is *my* moment. I've been planning this for weeks and you've ruined it with your silly strutting. You're a nightmare to direct. I resign!' The distraught elf stamped into a corner, where he was quietly comforted by a friend.

Bad Christmas looked daggers at him, sat down, composed himself and turned back to the camera with a broad smile.

'Dearest people, I shall shortly appear before you to receive all my lovely presents. You are so kind, so thoughtful, and I thank you from the heart of my bottom. I command you to form an orderly queue and in two hours' time I shall appear, seated upon my Christmas throne, and you may bring your gifts and come and worship me. Thank you so much, and goodnight.'

'It's daytime,' muttered one of the elves.

'Look out there,' said Bad Christmas. 'Can you see the sun? No. Is it dark? Yes. SO IT MUST BE NIGHT TIME, THEN, YOU STUPID IDIOT. STOP CORRECTING ME OR I'LL SHOVE YOU ON TOP OF THE CHRISTMAS TREE!'

Bad Christmas took a deep breath, smoothed his hair and beamed at the other elves. 'Was I good? Was I wonderful?'

'Yes, Chief of Chiefs. Very good, very wonderful.'

An elf sitting at Mission Control swung round. 'Control reporting in. Father Christmas has now docked in Bay One and Big Chief Elf has docked the sleigh in Bay Two. Big Chief reports the capture of two further prisoners.'

Bad Christmas gave a happy sigh. 'Oh, goody,' he murmured. 'Such power. Such glory. Throw the whole lot in the laboratory. I must go and gloat over them. I do so like gloating.'

In the laboratory Father Christmas had been isolated in one cage while the others were herded into a larger cell. Mrs Christmas gazed sadly at her husband.

'He's just not himself,' she murmured. 'It's like he's been hypnotized or something. Eek!' She leaped back as Boo-Boo appeared right in front of her face, closely followed by Bad Christmas.

'My dear woman, the word you're looking for is "puddified". He has been contaminated with Sticky Matter – the same Sticky Matter that I have used to make every Christmas pudding in the world.'

'So that's what happened to the others!' Lewis

cried. 'They ate the puddings and got puddified.'

Bad Christmas rolled his eyes. 'Oh, hooray, you've put two and two together at last. It's only taken you three days. And to think humans are supposed to be the brainiest creatures on the planet. A goldfish could have told you it was the puddings.'

 Here is our chief science explainerifier, Professor Bump-Pumbitt:

'No, no, no! This is just silly now. A goldfish certainly could not explain anything because it does not have the right kind of vocal chords. As for humans being the brainiest creatures on the planet – well, I sometimes wonder. You quite wear me out with your constant questioning. I'm not going to explain anything else. In fact, I'm going home. Goodbye!'

Amy gripped the bars of the cage. 'Everyone eats Christmas pudding on Christmas Day,' she squeaked.

'I don't,' muttered Lewis, but Bad Christmas wasn't listening. He was far too busy being pleased with himself.

'Exactly, and now almost everyone on Earth has been puddified and they are all in my control – millions, billions, trillions. Isn't it wonderful!'

'You're a maniac!' shouted Miss Comet.

'I do like it when you tell me off,' chortled Bad Christmas. 'Isn't it fun being naughty, Boo-Boo?'

'Are you going to leave the whole world zombified forever?' demanded Mrs Christmas.

'Let me think. Boo-Boo says YES! I say NO. Boo-Boo says YES! I say NO! So the answer is . . . YES!'

'But you must have an antidote that removes the effects.'

'Of course,' repeated Bad Christmas.

'What is it?' asked Lewis.

Bad Christmas raised his eyebrows. 'Goodness me, you're almost quite bright. Fortunately I am certainly not stupid; shan't tell. Now then, must get on. Bring me Father Christmas's lovely coat. It will soon be time for me to take his place and I shall collect all my prezzies. Oh, sweet victory! As for this lot,' he added, gazing fondly at Miss Comet and her companions, 'prepare to puddify them! Ho ho ho ho ho!'

Will the whole world be puddified? Read on, before it's too late!

SIX AND
AN EXTRA BIT:
IN BAY TWO . . .

The elves had left the sleigh. They were definitely
in the mood for food and were determined not
to miss out. 'I know what will happen,' grumbled
Big Chief. 'The others will get there first and wolf
it all. They're pigs, that's what.'

'Yes, Chief, pigs,' echoed three of the team.
The fourth scratched his head.

''Scuse me, Chief,' he began, 'but if they're
wolfing it down then surely they must be wolves?
If they're pigs they'd be pigging it, but you said –'

'Shut up!' yelled Big Chief Elf. 'Just for that you
can stay on guard here!'

'I was only saying. I mean, wolves and pigs,
they're different creatures.'

'SHUT UP!' bellowed Big Chief. 'You stand

right there and don't move until I send further orders. Understood?' The elf sighed and stood beside the sleigh, while the others went off singing and laughing.

Inside his sack, Rufus heard the door slide shut. He waited and listened, but all he could hear was the shuffling of a reindeer's hoof and the elf-guard grumbling about bossy Big Chiefs who couldn't tell a pig from an elephant. This was useful because the mutterings gave Rufus a rough idea of the elf's position.

'Keep still and quiet,' he whispered to Dylan and Freya, hoping they could hear him.

Rufus slowly opened his sack and climbed out. He raised his head until he could see over the high front seat. The guard had his back to Rufus and was still mumbling to himself.

Rufus grinned. All he had to do was climb over the seat, throw himself at the guard and overpower him. He lifted one long leg over the seat and then the other. Rufus moved forward,

getting into a crouching
position, ready to hurl
himself upon the guard.

'Anyway,' the guard
muttered, 'they can't just
leave me here to starve. I bet
there's food on that sleigh
somewhere.'

AND HE TURNED ROUND!

In an instant Rufus found a Blatter-Splatter
pointing straight at him.

'Oh my, I've caught a big
one!' cried the delighted elf.
'Hold it right there, mister,
or I'll puddify you. Big Chief
is going to love
me. Whoopee!
An' I don't
have to stand
here no more cos
I shall now have

to deliver you to the big boss. Keep your hands in the air and climb down. Take it easy and don't try anything. Now, quick march!'

The elf prodded a crestfallen Rufus in the back and began to march him towards the door. The elf was only halfway there when a thunderbolt ploughed into his back, sending him plunging to the floor, desperately trying to fight off a mad Dylan, who was pummelling him. The Sticky Matter gun let off a blast and a stream of gunge shot across the chamber and hit one of the reindeer.

Rufus threw himself into the struggle and between them Dylan and his father overpowered the elf. Rufus seized the weapon and, smiling broadly, he and Dylan high-fived each other. Freya stood on the sleigh and clapped them both.

'It's like being in a film!' she cried excitedly, jumping down. 'Can we tie him up?'

Rufus shook his head. 'He's going to show us round the *Death Pudding*.'

Freya suddenly let out a sad 'Oh!'. She had noticed the reindeer that had been bombarded with Sticky Matter. 'Look, she's – weird. She's alive but sort of not alive.'

The elf sneered. 'She's been puddified,' and he explained about Sticky Matter.

'Surely there's a way of depuddifying her?' suggested Rufus, and again the elf sneered.

'Only the big boss knows that and you're going to have problems even getting to see him because there's loads of us elves on board and there's only three of you and two of you's little kids and it only takes one tiny drop of Sticky Matter and you'll be puddified yourselves. I'd give up now if I were you.'

'Well, you're not us,' snapped Freya. 'So you can be quiet or we'll puddify you!'

'What do we do now?' Dylan asked, glancing at his father.

'I guess the elves have taken Miss Comet to Bad Christmas and he'll be at the controls of this space pudding, or whatever it is.'

Freya bit her nails anxiously. 'What do we do?' It was a question Rufus had been asking himself ever since the sleigh had been captured.

'We must find Miss Comet and rescue her.'

'What about the others?' asked Dylan, and his father blushed.

'Yes, them as well, of course.'

Freya nudged Dylan and raised her eyebrows.

'What?' he answered and she rolled her eyes.

'Nothing,' she murmured, giving him an innocent smile.

The elf began to laugh and shake his head. 'You're mad! Don't you understand? This ship is crawling with armed elves. You'll be puddified in seconds.'

Rufus waved the gun at him. 'We've got one too. Now, tell us, what do you use to stop Sticky Matter from sticking to you?'

'We don't shoot each other! What would be the point in that? There isn't anything. I told you, once it sticks to you, you're done for.'

'We need non-stick armour,' Dylan murmured half-heartedly, and his father's jaw dropped.

'What? Non-stick armour? What a brilliant idea! You're a brainbox, Dyl!'

'Dad, it was a joke. There's no such thing.'

'On the contrary,' Rufus grinned. 'You have given me a good idea, but first we must rescue Miss Comet.'

'And the others,' added Freya, nudging Dylan again.

'Of course,' muttered Rufus. He turned to the elf-guard. 'Take us to the laboratory,' he ordered.

'You fools! You're all going to die!' hissed the elf.

'Then you'll be the first to go, won't you?' Rufus pointed out. 'Go on – move!'

SIX AND A TWEENY-WEENY BIT: MEANWHILE DOWN ON THE BLUE PLANET . . .

Bad Christmas was almost delirious with happiness. He had taken an armed platoon with him down to Earth, but it was quite unnecessary. The world had done exactly as it had been ordered and there they stood – a long, endless line of silent zombies, holding their gifts as they patiently waited for Father Christmas to appear.

And there he was! At least, Bad Christmas was there, wearing his brother's red coat. He even had Boo-Boo dressed in a little red cap. He walked solemnly to the throne that had been specially built for this grand moment and admired it from every angle. He stroked its polished wooden arms. He caressed the plush back of the red leather seat, set between mahogany pillars, each one topped off with a carved Christmas pudding. Finally he sat down and looked at the snaking queue.

'Dear, dear people,' he crooned. 'You are so wonderful. You may approach and bestow your gifts. Come, I am ready to receive.'

One by one they came, each with a gift. Of course the gift had originally been for them. The presents still had labels saying things like:

Happy Christmas to Jenny, from Uncle Bill

For little Sam, with love from Mum and Dad

This is for Alice, from her adoring hubbie, Jack

Bad Christmas didn't bother with the labels. He tore at the wrapping paper and pulled out the presents one by one. 'A Barbie doll! Lovely! Thank you. Next!' He threw the doll over his shoulder. 'A train set! Whoo whooo! Thank you. Next!' The train flew over his shoulder. 'Ooh, Boo-Boo, look here – a red bra and pants. Just my size, hee hee! Next!'

And so it went on. And on and on and on. You might have thought that Bad Christmas would soon tire of it all, but he didn't. He sat on the throne, giggling with delight, opening present after present. This could go on for days.

SEVEN: ☆ ☆
AN EXCITING ☆ ☆
MOMENT ON THE
DEATH PUDDING . . .

On their way to the laboratory the Rescue Team
managed to overpower two armed elves, and
trebled their own firepower. Freya held a Sticky
Matter gun in both hands, gazing at it in disbelief.

'Wow! This is amazing!'

Dylan handled his weapon rather more
gingerly. 'I don't like it,' he muttered.

'Pow! Pow!' went Freya, pointing and
pretending. Rufus looked from Dylan to Freya and
back to his son.

'You'd better watch out, Dyl, she's dangerous.
OK. Here we are. Ready? There could be a lot of
guards in here, so watch out. Elf-friend here can
lead the charge.'

'But they'll puddify me!' protested the elf.

'Then you'd better make sure they don't,' Rufus
suggested. 'Three, two, one – let's go!'

The team burst into the lab. Four startled
guards leaped away from their desks and ran for
their weapons but they were too slow. Zip! Zap!
Zop! Sticky Matter criss-crossed the room and
zombified them in their tracks.

Rufus raced across to the cage and smashed
it open. Mrs Christmas, the
children and Miss Comet
tumbled out. Rufus
caught Miss
Comet in his
arms.

'Oh!' she gasped.

'Goodness me, you took your time,' complained
Mrs Christmas. 'Honestly, I have never had to
play so many games of I-spy in my whole life.
And Miss Comet wouldn't stop asking about . . .
Miss Comet, what are you doing? Ah. Yes, I see.
Children, turn away at once. I think Rufus and
Miss Comet are having A Moment.'

'A moment?' Lewis rolled his eyes and went to
Dylan. 'Huh. She's done nothing but talk about
your dad all the time we've been locked up.'

Meanwhile Mrs Christmas had set her husband
free, not that it did much good. His eyes were
glassy and lifeless and he simply stood there in
T-shirt and boxer shorts.

'Don't just stand there, jellybean. Do
something! Hello? Is anybody in? Ooh, you
always were an exasperating old walrus. Go
on, then, you can stay there for all I care.' But
of course Mrs Christmas did care and she was
already muttering to herself about finding an

antidote. 'Maybe it's on the computer. Let's have a look.' She whizzed through files. 'There must be an antidote.'

'Nobody knows the antidote,' sneered the elf-guard.

'Oh, stop carping, misery guts!' Mrs Christmas cried, spinning round in her chair and jabbing him with a knitting needle.

'Aaargh!' He leaped into the air, clutching his behind, and then ran whimpering into a corner.

The others stared at her in astonishment. She shrugged. 'He was getting on my nerves, quarrelling with everything I said. Honestly. Oh, look, here's the recipe for Sticky Matter.'

They gathered round and studied the list. 'Molasses, raisins, flour, eggs, sugar, peel and, last of all, sprouts. Sprouts? And look, down here, underlined, it says, "DON'T FORGET SPROUTS, JUST IN CASE". You don't put sprouts in Christmas pudding.'

'Huh, it always tastes like sprouts,' said Lewis.

'Revolting.'

'There are boxes and boxes of sprouts over there,' Miss Comet said. 'I thought they were for feeding the animals.'

'They can't be feeding animals with them,' said Amy. 'These are all unopened.'

Mrs Christmas tore open the top box and pulled out a sprout. 'Time for a little experiment,' she declared. 'Now then, jellybean, I want you to eat this. It might do you some good. It certainly won't do any harm. I'm sorry I don't have time

to cook it. You'll have to eat it raw. Open your mouth. There. Stand back, everyone. Who knows what might happen!'

Father Christmas chewed the raw vegetable. He blinked. He shook his head. He stretched. He stretched his body and yawned, as if he had just woken from a deep sleep. He noticed Mrs Christmas for the first time.

'What are you staring at me like that for?' he grunted. 'Where am I? What's going on? Who are all these people? What are these animals doing here? Why is that elf dressed like a tartan monkey? What are those children doing with guns?'

'Stop!' cried Mrs Christmas, almost crying with laughter. 'Come here, you big bumbling bumblebag.' And she gave him a huge hug. 'Do you know what the antidote to Sticky Matter is? Sprouts. You ate a raw sprout.'

'I can't have. I don't like sprouts. I don't like cooked sprouts, let alone raw ones.'

It took a few minutes to put Father Christmas in the picture and he slowly grew more and more angry. 'Right,' he declared, 'what we need is a plan.'

'We already have one,' Rufus announced.

'Oh. Is it any good?'

'It's the best we can come up with. We're going to have to storm the Command Centre and take over the *Death Pudding*. But before we do that we must visit the kitchen.'

'Oh, good, I'm hungry. I've only eaten a sprout all day,' grumbled Father Christmas, still finding shreds in his mouth. 'It tastes horrible.'

They slipped along the corridor. Carefully peering through the kitchen door, Rufus could see that the only elves in sight were three washer-uppers, busy at a sink. He sneaked inside and before they knew it they had a Sticky Matter gun pointing at them.

'Hello!' smiled Rufus. 'Yes, do please put your hands in the air. Rescue Team, collect up every bit of non-stick stuff you can find: pots, pans, baking

trays – the lot. Mr and Mrs Christmas, perhaps
you could tie up this clutch of elves.'

While the others hunted for non-stick cookware,
Mrs Christmas finally gave up trying to stop her
cardigan unravelling and used ALL her wool to
tie up the elves – and very pretty they looked too.

The children and Rufus got to work on
converting kitchen equipment into armour. They
taped baking tins across their chests and strapped
frying pans to their arms and legs. They put
saucepans on their heads. Father Christmas's
head was so big he had to use a stew pot.

Rufus surveyed his strange army. 'It's time to
take control. Follow me, troops.'

It didn't take long to reach the seat of power. As
they gathered outside the Command Centre Miss
Comet slipped a hand into Rufus's. 'Be careful,
won't you?' she said. Behind them Lewis was
pretending to be sick.

'Oh, please!' he complained.

'Stop it,' said Amy. 'I think it's lovely.'

'I think it's lovely!' echoed Lewis in a sing-song voice. 'Yuck!'

'Battle stations, everyone!' ordered Rufus. 'Are you ready? CHAAAAARGE!'

SEVEN AND IT'S *EVEN MORE EXCITING THAN THE LAST BIT: THE COMMAND CENTRE* . . .

It sounded as if a truck full of dustbins had fallen down a cliff. It was the noise of umpteen non-stick pots, pans, trays and saucepan lids banging together as the Magnificent Eight came tearing into the Command Centre.

Big Chief leaped from the Seat of High Command, where he had been lazing with his feet

screamed, as the elves ran for their Sticky Matter
Blatter-Splatters. Streams of dark brown goo were
soon slicing across the room.

The eight warriors threw themselves to the
ground, just as they had seen heroes do in
countless movies. They tried rolling over, but it's
very difficult to roll with several saucepans and
baking trays tied round your middle. They soon
found it better to throw themselves down and slide,
although it made the most awful screeching sound.

'Yah! Eat Sticky Matter, suckers!' yelled Father
Christmas, felling three elves with a single blast.
For a second he seemed very surprised at himself,

before grinning wickedly and carrying on.

Amy was overpowered by several elves. They were carrying her away when they suddenly came face to face with Miss Comet wearing her sternest face.

'Put her down, at once!' she ordered. And they did.

'Sorry, miss,' said the lead elf, before turning round and rushing back into battle.

Amy looked up at Miss Comet and whispered a shy 'thank you'. Then she uttered a blood-curdling scream and tore back into the fray.

Miss Comet shouted across to Rufus, deep in his own battle with the elves. 'It's just like break time!'

Meanwhile Father Christmas and his wife stood back to back, fighting off endless elf-attacks, he with his gun and she with her knitting needles, jabbing left and right. There were moments when the Magnificent Eight seemed to be surrounded by gun-happy elves and it would be impossible to survive the criss-cross stream of Sticky Matter that filled the room. Time and time again the Rescue Team were hit, but the puddings slid harmlessly off the non-stick surfaces of their armour.

Dylan and Freya were edging along either side of the room, moving towards the Seat of High Command. Big Chief was standing there, bellowing commands to his troops. All at once he leaped down and hurried over to a small instrument panel.

'He's trying to send a warning message to Bad Christmas,' yelled Freya. 'Stop him!'

There was too much going on for either of them to get a sight line on the elf. Dylan was nearest. It was down to him. He swallowed. There was a seething throng of elves between him and Big Chief, but he had no choice. He was only going to get one go at this. He took a deep breath, gritted his teeth, put his head down, closed his eyes tight and charged forward.

BANG! BIFF! WALLOP! KRRANG! THUD!
BLIPP! BOYOINNGG!

Elves bounced off the charging battering ram

like peas pinging off a wall of steel. Dylan opened
his eyes and saw the look of shock on Big Chief
Elf's face as he crashed straight into him and a
strenuous wrestling match began. They wriggled
and rolled and biffed, baffed and boffed until

Big Chief was sitting triumphantly astride an exhausted Dylan.

'Pipsqueak!' hissed Big Chief. Then Freya landed on his head and knocked him cold.

With Big Chief captured, the remaining elves threw down their weapons and surrendered. The Magnificent Eight gathered together with much hand-slapping, back-thumping and hugging. (The hugging bit was only Rufus and Miss Comet. Freya thought she heard a kiss too, but Dylan said it was only their baking trays clashing.)

The awesome *Death Pudding* had fallen into their hands and Rufus nodded with satisfaction. 'Now we must tackle Bad Christmas down on Earth.'

Miss Comet smiled. 'I've been thinking about that. I have a little plan.'

SEVEN
AND THE END:
RETURN TO EARTH . . .

'How lovely!' sighed Bad Christmas. 'A steam iron. Just what I always wanted.' He chucked the iron over his shoulder. 'Next! Ah, look at this: curling tongs. Won't we look stylish, Boo-Boo? Next!'

The endless line of zombified present-givers shuffled forward, watched from a safe distance by Rufus and the Rescue Team. They had immobilized the *Death Pudding* before they left and Rufus had the ignition key safe in his pocket. The elves had been zombified for the time being. Only raw sprouts would bring them back to themselves.

Father Christmas, still in his underwear, (giant spotted boxer shorts and a T-shirt with a slogan on the front saying CHRISTMAS IS COMING

and another on the back: CHRISTMAS IS GOING), was grinding his teeth. 'How dare my brother parade around like that, wearing my special coat? And how dare he make people give him presents? It's outrageous.'

Mrs Christmas agreed. 'I know, jellybean.

It shouldn't be allowed. But look at all the guards he's got.' She turned to Miss Comet. 'What's the plan?'

Miss Comet nodded. 'I think we should join the queue. We'll have to remove our armour and hide our weapons under our clothes. The queue moves forward, and when we get to Bad Christmas – bingo! He's suddenly surrounded! The elves will have to surrender.'

Rufus was already in agreement. Father Christmas frowned a lot and scratched his head, while the children looked at the adults and waited for them to make up their minds.

'Agreed,' Father Christmas said gruffly.

With weapons hidden from view, they joined the queue. It wasn't difficult to penetrate the line of shuffling zombies and soon the adventurers were shuffling along too, with Rufus in the lead. Their heads were bowed and they looked for all the world as if they had been puddified.

In front of Rufus was a young girl. She was

about five or six and was holding a present close to her chest. Rufus found himself getting very angry as he thought about this poor child who had been puddified and was now having to obey a megalomaniac. He couldn't wait to get his hands on Bad Christmas.

The queue edged forward. Rufus whispered back to Miss Comet. 'We're almost there. Get ready.' Their hands tightened on the Splatter guns.

The little girl in front of Rufus had reached the grinning, swollen figure of Bad Christmas. 'Next!' he called. The girl stepped forward and held out her gift.

'It's my teddy,' she said shyly.

Bad Christmas was astonished. The girl had spoken! Zombies weren't supposed to speak! He gazed at her intently. She looked back at him, her eyes bright and shiny. The truth suddenly dawned on him.

SHE HADN'T BEEN PUDDIFIED!

YET HERE SHE WAS, WITH A PRESENT
FOR HIM!!

Bad Christmas leaned forward and took the
little teddy. It was warm and soft. 'How lovely,' he
murmured. 'Surely this is your teddy?'

The girl nodded. 'Yes. But it's OK, I've got
three more at home. This is only my second best
one. It's not my first.'

Bad Christmas didn't seem to hear. 'You're

giving me your teddy?'

'Yes.'

'Why are you giving me a present?'

'I saw you on television and you looked sad and I thought that's how I feel when I haven't got my teddy at night, so I brought you one.'

Bad Christmas swallowed and blinked quickly, several times. 'Do you think it will work?' he asked huskily.

'It works for me,' the little girl answered.

'Oh. Thank you,' he muttered. 'Nobody has ever given me a present before. I mean, not

actually *given* me one. All these,' he went on, casting an eye over the huge pile behind him, 'they're just tokens. But now I have your teddy. Look, Boo-Boo, you have a new friend.'

The girl smiled and walked off, while Bad Christmas sat there hugging the teddy and the tartan beanie. Tears had welled up in his eyes, and as the Magnificent Eight prepared to surround and seize him, his shoulders hunched up and he started to cry.

'What do we do?' asked Rufus, completely confused.

Father Christmas stamped his feet crossly. 'The trouble is, it's very difficult to get angry with someone who's upset, even when it's your own evil big brother. I don't know. What do you think we should do?' he asked his wife.

'Well, I'm certainly not going to take his teddy away,' she said. 'Miss Comet, what do you think?'

But even Miss Comet was stumped. 'He does look very upset,' she murmured, because although

Miss Comet could be very strict when necessary she actually had a heart as soft as the best fudge there is.

There was a long, snuffling and whuffling noise as Bad Christmas sniffed and blew his nose. He looked up at the people standing in front of him and suddenly recognized them. But he didn't jump up and call for the guards. He held out the teddy instead. 'A child gave me this. She *gave* it to *me*. It's a *gift*!'

'That's what Christmas is about,' Father Christmas said gruffly. 'Now then, what are you going to do about all these people you've puddified?'

'Oh, I just have to sproutify them. Sprouts are the antidote.'

'We know,' Mrs Christmas said smugly. 'Because we went on your computer and we worked it out for ourselves.'

'Of course,' said Bad Christmas, with great tiredness in his voice. 'My little brother – you've depuddified him.' He turned to Father Christmas. 'I suppose you'd like your robe back?'

'Hmmm. I'm not sure. Since you're dressed for the part maybe you should finish the job. Then I can have a day off and Mrs Christmas and I can take a holiday. We've never been able to holiday at Christmas before. Then next year I'll be Father Christmas again, and you can do it the year after that, and so on. Nobody will know.'

Bad Christmas's eyes widened. 'You'd let me do that? After everything I've done to you?' Father Christmas coughed and frowned and nodded. 'Then that's two gifts I've been given today!' cried Bad Christmas. 'I wish I had something I could give.'

Dylan pushed forward. 'Excuse me,' he said. 'You have twenty-four children at my school to depuddify, plus all the rest of the people on the planet AND the animals in the laboratory on the *Death Pudding*. Not to mention all these presents to give back.'

Bad Christmas jumped up. 'Yes! And I shall start straight away.'

So it was that everyone got dezombified and everything ended happily after all. For a short while everyone wondered what to do about the *Death Pudding*. There were suggestions that it could be turned into an adventure playground, but there were an awful lot of children who said they didn't want to look at another Christmas pudding after what had happened to them, and they certainly didn't want to play in one.

In the end the air force came along and bombed it to bits and the whole thing went up in smoke and flames, while they watched from a safe distance.

Miss Comet laughed. 'Look, Dylan, it's just like the picture you drew in class.'

Dylan quietly asked his father if he was going to marry his teacher. 'Because it wouldn't be fair. It would be like being in school all day and all night. There'd be no escape,' he complained.

But he didn't mind, not really. He was already thinking chicken and mayonnaise, cheese and tomato . . . the days of disaster sandwiches could be over.

Sound FX: Happy, cheerful wedding-march-type music, and the sound of Lewis pretending to be sick.

Ask Jeremy

Of all the books you have written, which one is your favourite?

I loved writing both **KRAZY KOW SAVES THE WORLD – WELL, ALMOST** and **STUFF**, my first book for teenagers. Both these made me laugh out loud while I was writing and I was pleased with the overall result in each case. I also love writing the stories about Nicholas and his daft family – **MY DAD**, **MY MUM**, **MY BROTHER** and so on.

If you couldn't be a writer what would you be?

Well, I'd be pretty fed up for a start, because writing was the one thing I knew I wanted to do from the age of nine onward. But if I DID have to do something else, I would love to be either an accomplished pianist or an artist of some sort. Music and art have played a big part in my whole life and I would love to be involved in them in some way.

What's the best thing about writing stories?

Oh dear – so many things to say here! Getting paid for making things up is pretty high on the list! It's also something you do on your own, inside your own head – nobody can interfere with that. The only boss you have is yourself. And you are creating something that nobody else has made before you. I also love making my readers laugh and want to read more and more.

Did you ever have a nightmare teacher?
(And who was your best ever?)

My nightmare at primary school was Mrs Chappell, long since dead. I knew her secret – she was not actually human. She was a Tyrannosaurus rex in disguise. She taught me for two years when I was in Y5 and Y6, and we didn't like each other at all. My best ever was when I was in Y3 and Y4. Her name was Miss Cox, and she was the one who first encouraged me to write stories. She was brilliant. Sadly, she is long dead too.

When you were a kid you used to play kiss-chase. Did you always do the chasing or did anyone ever chase you?!

I usually did the chasing, but when I got chased, I didn't bother to run very fast! Maybe I shouldn't admit to that! We didn't play kiss-chase at school – it was usually played during holidays. If we had tried playing it at school we would have been in serious trouble. Mind you, I seemed to spend most of my time in trouble of one sort or another, so maybe it wouldn't have mattered that much.

Woofy hi! I'm Streaker, the fastest dog in the world. My owner, Trevor, thinks he can train me to obey him. The trouble is even I don't know what I'm going to do next! I don't know what SIT or STOP mean, and I do get into some big scrapes. We almost got arrested once! This is the first book about me and it's almost as funny and fast as I am!

LAUGH YOUR SOCKS OFF WITH

THE HUNDRED-MILE-AN-HOUR DOG

Available Now!

* * * * * * * * * * * * * * * * * *

I'm Jamie. I am going to be the world's greatest film director when I grow up. I'm trying to make a film about a cartoon cow I've invented called KRAZY KOW. However, making a film isn't as easy as you might think. How was I to know everyone would see the bit where I caught my big sister snogging Justin? How was I to know the exploding strawberries would make quite so much mess? How was I to know my big bro's football kit would turn pink? And why did everyone have to blame ME?

LAUGH YOUR SOCKS OFF WITH

KRAZY KOW SAVES THE WORLD – WELL, ALMOST

Available Now!

Puffin by Post

Invasion of the Christmas Puddings – Jeremy Strong

If you have enjoyed this book and want to read more,
then check out these other great Puffin titles.
You can order any of the following books direct with Puffin by Post: